Copyright © 2012 by Todd H. Goldman
All rights reserved. / CIP data is available.
Published in the United States 2012 by
🍎 Blue Apple Books, 515 Valley Street, Maplewood, NJ 07040
www.blueapplebooks.com
First Edition   05/12   Printed in Dongguan, China
ISBN: 978-1-60905-203-4
10 9 8 7 6 5 4 3 2 1

Todd H. Doodler

Honey Bear's
Blue Bathing Suit

BLUE 🍎 APPLE

Honey Bear's birthday
was in two weeks.

She planned a beach party
for her friends.

Honey Bear was super excited
and made invitations for her guests.

YOU ARE INVITED TO

HONEY BEAR'S BIRTHDAY PARTY EXTRAVAGANZA!

ICE CREAM!

CAKE!

BALLOONS!

GAMES!

BRING A TOWEL AND A BATHING SUIT.
GET READY TO GET **WET!**
AND DON'T FORGET THE SUNSCREEN.

TIME: 2 PM
PLACE: SEASHELL BEACH

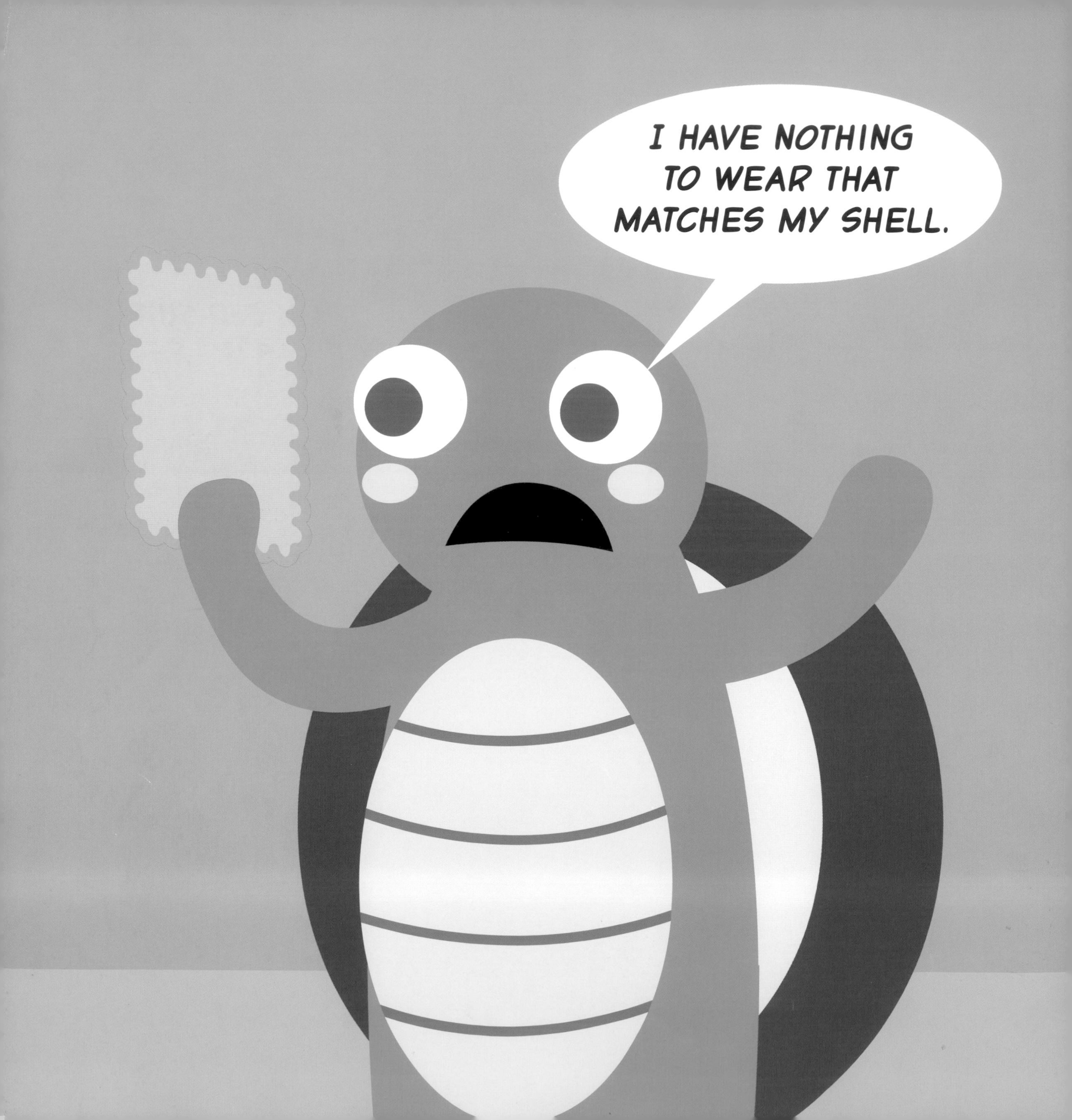
I HAVE NOTHING TO WEAR THAT MATCHES MY SHELL.

When they stopped for pizza, they met Cougar, Beaver, and Deer.

LET'S CHIP IN AND BUY HER SOMETHING COOL.
GREAT IDEA!
GOOD THINKING.
HEY, WHAT SHOULD WE GET?

LET'S GET SOME BEACHY STUFF!

Big Foot said he would carry all of the presents in a beach bag since he was the strongest.

Beaver said he would bring a big bow to put on the beach bag.

Rabbit said he would bake the cake— carrot cake, of course!

NEAT-O!

After buying Honey Bear's gift,
Big Foot held up the birthday card, a big surfboard,
for everyone to sign.

HOORAY!

HAPPY BIRTHDAY,
HONEY BEAR

When they found Honey Bear,
she was setting up for volleyball.

Big Foot won the first
game of volleyball
for his team . . .

with a giant spike
at the net!

Then Honey Bear announced
the scavenger hunt.

WHOEVER COLLECTS
THE MOST SHELLS
(NO BROKEN ONES)
IS THE WINNER!

When the scavenger hunt was over,
Honey Bear counted everyone's shells.
Turtle won with 23.

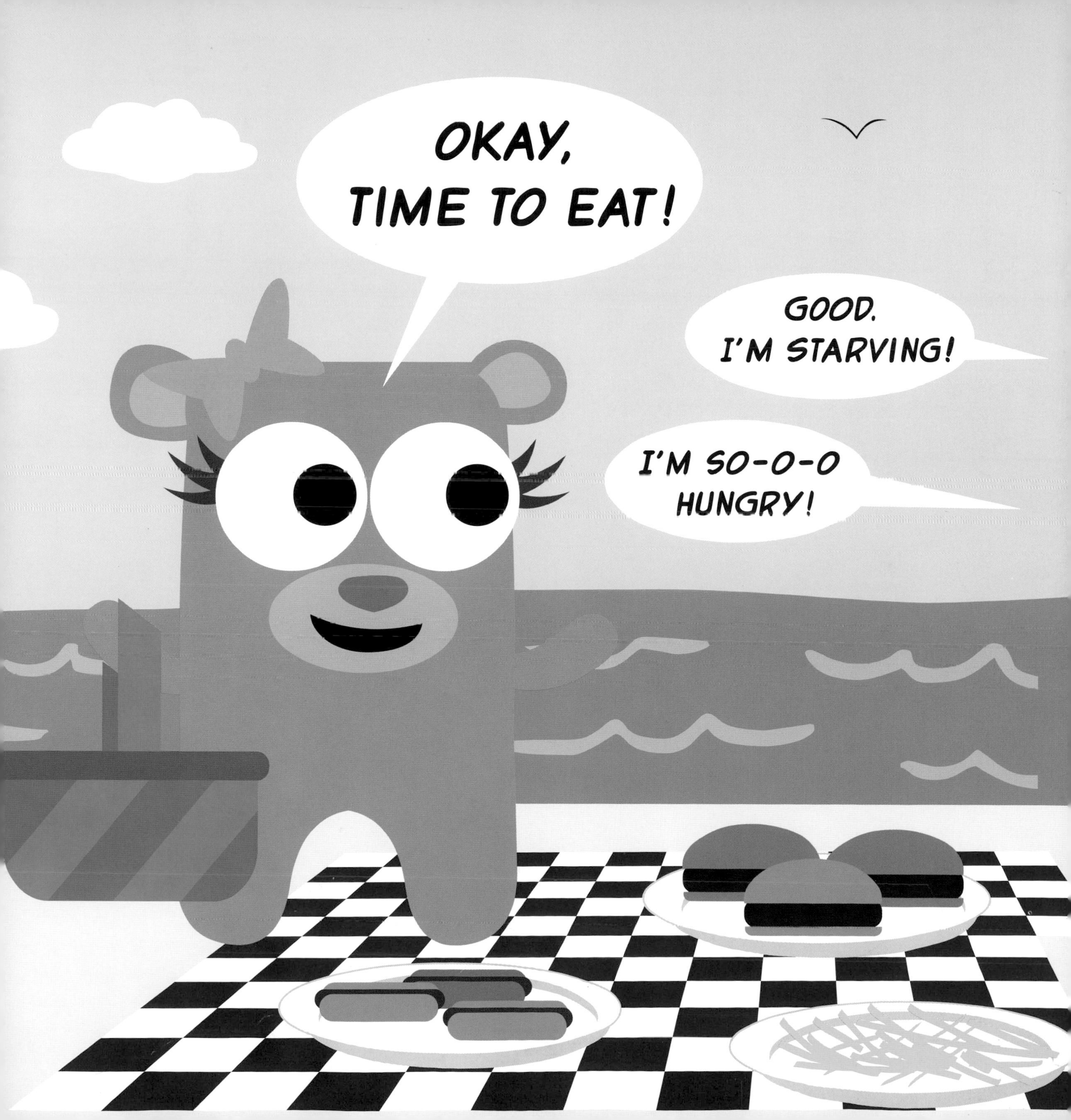
OKAY, TIME TO EAT!
GOOD. I'M STARVING!
I'M SO-O-O HUNGRY!

Everyone filled up on hot dogs, hamburgers, and fries.

DELICIOUS!

I'M STUFFED!

I CAN'T EAT ANOTHER BITE!

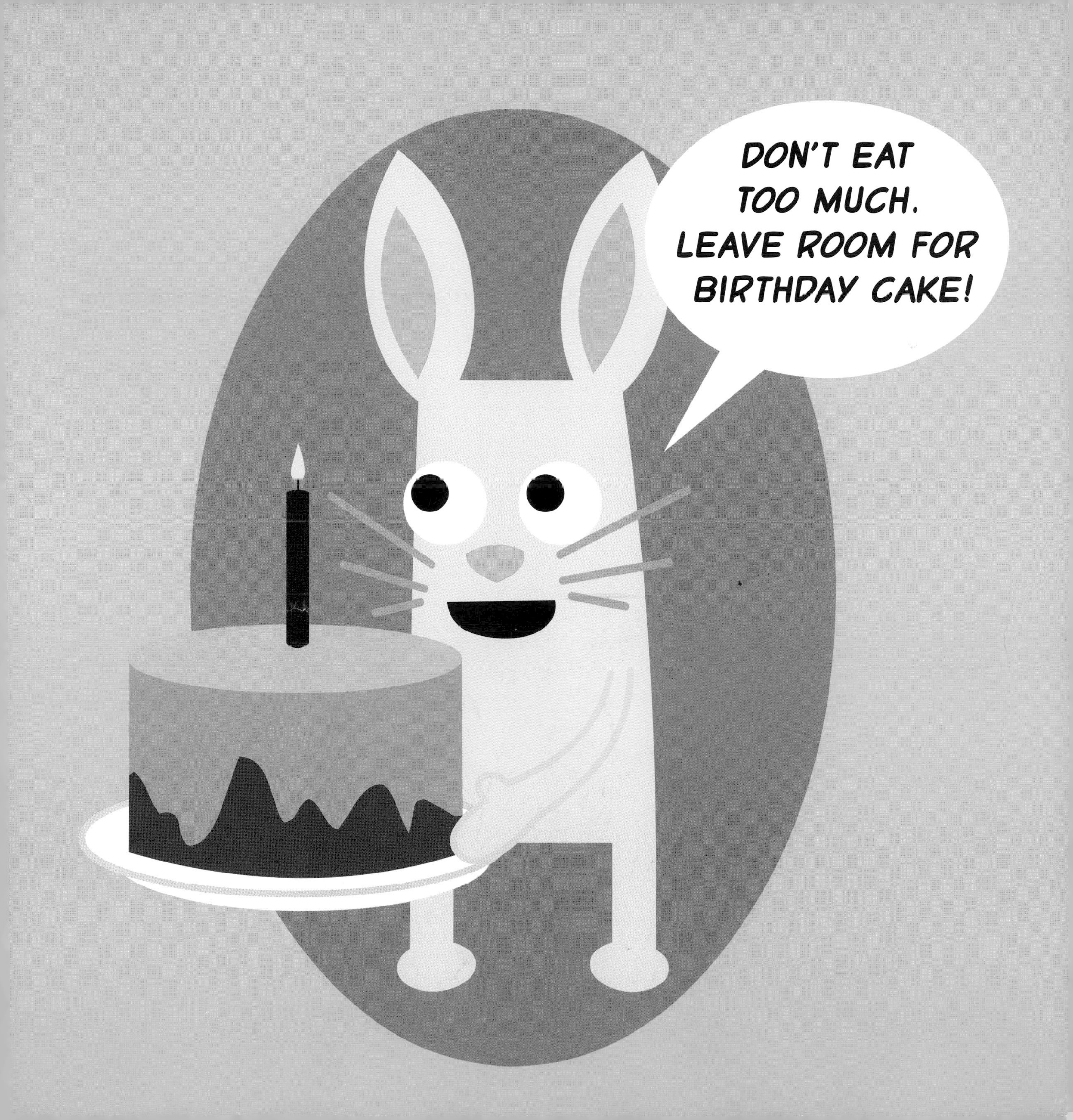
DON'T EAT
TOO MUCH.
LEAVE ROOM FOR
BIRTHDAY CAKE!

Rabbit cut the cake and gave everyone a slice.

Rabbit left the last, and biggest, slice
for the birthday girl herself . . . Honey Bear.

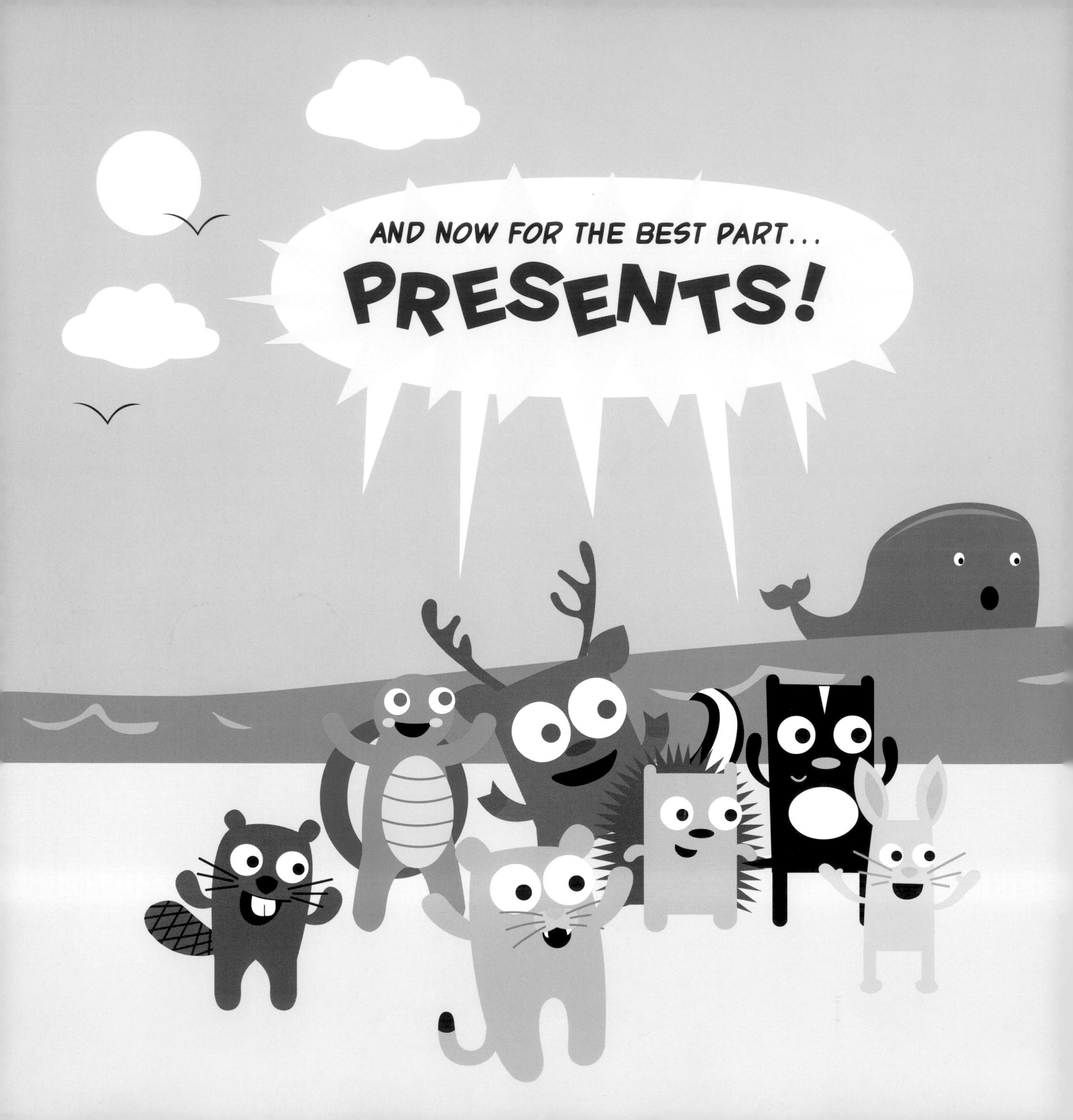
AND NOW FOR THE BEST PART...
PRESENTS!

Big Foot handed Honey Bear the beach bag
with her presents and gave her instructions:

TAKE THIS
TO THE
LOCKER ROOM
AND COME
BACK OUT WITH
EVERYTHING.

I CAN'T WAIT TO SEE WHAT SHE LOOKS LIKE.

While Honey Bear was in the locker room, everyone put on their bathing suits.

I HOPE SHE LIKES OUR PRESENT.

I HAVE SAND IN MY SUIT!

THIS SUIT IS A PERFECT FIT!
THANKS, EVERYBODY. I LOVE ALL MY PRESENTS!

Everyone got wet and jumped the waves.